Special thanks to:

My mother, Beatrice Elizabeth Bridges, for everything; my father and his wife, Jerome and Joann Bridges, for their continued encouragement; and Ayanna Niambi for bringing this story to life with her brilliant artistry. Finally, a special thanks to my daughter, my muse – Asha Bridges, who is studying as an undergrad at Howard University, living out her dreams and following God's perfect plan for her life.

"My Favorite Color is Blue"

In Spirit Power and Truth Publishing, LLC
Columbus, OH

ISBN-10: 1523419164
ISBN-13: 978-1523419166

Meet the Author and the Illustrator—

Stephanie R. Bridges has wanted to become a published author since she was a child. It was not until she focused her writing on God that her dreams began to come true. Stephanie also writes short stories, songs, and poetry. She has a B.S. in Secondary English Education from The Ohio State University. Stephanie lives in Columbus, Ohio, with her children, and she wants nothing more than to share their stories with kids around the world.

Ayanna Niambi has a B.A. in Illustration and Animation from the Columbus College of Art and Design. She is a freelance artist that creates conceptual art, character, graphic and tattoo designs. Ayanna loves to create artwork around musical, fictional and pure imaginative inspiration. Ayanna also blogs and vlogs, has a passion for music, books and creativity in all forms. She has a grand entrepreneurial spirit.

For Nancy

My name is Asha, and I love school and the color blue.

Like the fish that swims in the deep blue sea,

in school is where I love to be.

Like the star that twinkles in midnight blue space,

I shine in the classroom with a bright smile on my face.

Like the bird that soars through the powder blue sky,

if I do my best, I believe I can fly.

Like the squash that wins the 1st place blue ribbon,

my mind grows with each new challenge I'm given.

Like the pupil that centers the bluest eye,

I stay focused on my goals and try, try, try.

Like the song chirped by the cheerful bluebird,

I heed the call of my inner nerd.

Like the pattern used to make my favorite blue jeans,

I follow the plan that leads to my dreams.

Like the speckles that make the robin's egg blue,

I am polka dotted with good, bad, bubbly and sad times too.

Like the girl who feels blue inside,

I know education can help people worldwide.

Like the student who sleeps in the blue room at night,

I thank God for the Good Book that teaches me right.

My name is Asha, and I love school and the color blue.

How about you?

What I Want to be When I Grow Up
By Asha   E. Bridges

Activist — I lead people!

Astronaut — I explore outer-space!

Author — I write books!

Designer — I create styles!

Horticulturist — I study plants!

Illustrator — I draw pictures!

Oceanographer — I explore sea-life!

Optometrist — I fix eyesight!

Pilot — I fly planes!

Photographer — I take pictures!

Preservationist — I save wildlife!

Teacher — I educate people!

ME — I love ME!

What do YOU want to be?

Made in the USA
Columbia, SC
29 June 2020